CHOOSE YOUR OWN ADVENTURE®

BROOKLYN MERMAID

BY C. E. SIMPSON

ILLUSTRATED BY GABHOR UTOMO

CHOOSECO
WAITSFIELD, VERMONT

Book design: Stacey Boyd, Big Eyedea Visual Design

For information regarding permission, write to:

CHOOSECO
P.O. Box 46
Waitsfield, Vermont 05673
www.cyoa.com

Publisher's Cataloging-In-Publication Data
Names: Simpson, C.E, author. | Utomo, Gabhor, illustrator.
Title: Brooklyn mermaid / Simpson, C.E. ; illustrated by Gabhor Utomo.
Description: Waitsfield, VT : Chooseco, 2022. | 30 b&w illustrations. |
Series: Choose your own adventure. | Audience: Ages 9-12. | Summary:
This interactive adventure book places the reader in the position of
an outlaw mermaid who must free family members imprisoned by the evil
Ruler of Atlantis by finding a lost relic.
Identifiers: ISBN 9781954232082 (softcover)
Subjects: LCSH: Mermaids -- Juvenile fiction. | Magic -- Juvenile fic-
tion. | Atlantis (Legendary place) -- Juvenile fiction. | Brooklyn (New
York, N.Y.) — Juvenile fiction. | LCGFT: plot-your-own stories. | BISAC:
JUVENILE FICTION / Action & Adventure / General. | JUVENILE FICTION /
Legends, Myths, Fables / General. | JUVENILE FICTION / Mermaids & Mer-
men.
Classification: LCC PZ7.1 S567 2022 | [FIC]--dc22

Printed in Canada

10 9 8 7 6 5 4 3 2 1

This adventure is dedicated to all climate activists, including you!

BEWARE and WARNING!

This book is different from other books.

You and YOU ALONE are in charge of what happens in this story.

There are dangers, choices, adventures, and consequences. YOU must use all of your numerous talents and much of your enormous intelligence. The wrong decision could end in disaster—even death. But don't despair. At any time, YOU can go back and make another choice, alter the path of your story, and change its result.

The year is 2083, and YOU are a mermaid, and a member of the rebel Merzood clan. Atlantis, your home, has fallen under the control of a corrupt Ruler, who wants to use your Merzood magic for evil. When he captures you and imprisons your family, he has a ransom demand: that you retrieve "the Eye," a lost Atlantean relic. Do you search for the Eye in Atlantis, or on land in nearby Brooklyn? Will you be able to find the Eye, rescue your family, and stop the Ruler from taking over the world?

Atlantis has fallen.

The clash between the Merzoods and the Atlantean elite forced the Ruler of Atlantis and his guards into hiding. After Atlantis fell, the Merzoods rebuilt their city off the coast of Brooklyn, safe from the wrath of Atlantis . . . or so they thought.

You were born into the rebellious Merzoods. Your name is Neruvid, but everyone calls you Neru. The Merzoods call you a seeker, which means you have a talent for puzzles, mazes, and searching the depths of the sea for mysterious objects to create inventions. And that is exactly what you're on your way to do when the mackerel finds you.

"Hey, where are you going?"

You swallow your frustration. Mackerel are notorious for tagging along when they're least wanted.

"I'm Finn," this one says brightly. You don't respond at first, but he keeps swimming after you.

"I'm going seeking," you finally say. "I got word from a clownfish in the reef that a Strider yacht sank a few fin flicks away from Merzood City."

"Striders?" Finn asks. You roll your eyes. This mackerel seems even slower than most of them.

Turn to the next page.

"The two-legged land creatures," you say curtly. "They leave behind all kinds of objects. My favorite is an encyclopedia that I found in the wreckage of a sailboat. The fragments are delicate, but I've been memorizing all the pages to learn as much as I can about the Striders. They're *fascinating*."

Finn seems to think about this for a minute. "If you're so interested in the Striders, what are you doing down here? You're a Merzood, aren't you?"

You sigh. "Yes. I live with my Auntie Echo and Auntie Quell, in a Hideaway in a sea cave on the outskirts of Merzood City. Just off the coast of Rockaway Beach in Brooklyn. Yes, I am a Merzood, and yes, that means if I go on land my tail and scales will change into legs and skin. But I still have to be careful. Striders are unpredictable. If I expose my true identity, I could risk the safety of my whole community. When the Atlanteans attacked Merzood City, many of the Merzoods escaped to the Strider world. I have relatives in Brooklyn, but I haven't met them yet. Sometimes—"

You pause, self-conscious all of a sudden. Finn doesn't need to know this, but sometimes, at night, you swim to Rockaway Beach and sit on the shore. You look at the lights of the Strider city. . . . It looks so magical. . . .

Go on to the next page.

You realize that the mackerel is talking, and you snap out of your reverie. This time he's chattering on about Merzood magic. "And I hear Merzoods can *read minds* and when they cast a spell it's *bright orange* and—"

"What?" you say. "No, none of that is true. Merzood magic always glows bright blue. And we can't read minds, but our magic takes many forms. Merzoods have been an active part of the ocean's ecosystems since the Jurassic period. Our magic runs as deep as the Mariana Trench." You feel a rush of pride, thinking about your community's rich history. "Merzood magic can help us find hidden places and treasures, and it can help with our aptitude for speaking the language of other sea creatures—that's how we're able to talk to each other right now. And it can also help create the bubble portals that my Aunties use to travel through space and time."

You stop talking again, suddenly anxious. The evil Ruler of Atlantis has always wanted to harness Merzood magic. His army of mutant guards are the fruits of his experiments, but he has never been able to truly replicate Merzood magic. Atlantean energy has a deep green glow, and it is usually used for destruction.

Turn to the next page.

4

The Merzoods live in harmony with the ocean. In the same way that trees synthesize oxygen, Merzoods use light like coral polyps; their scales conduct energy. The Merzoods haven't seen the Atlantean guards in a long time, but you know that if you spot their inky acid-green glow, they are close.

You and Finn continue to swim through Merzood City, and when you reach the city center, you pass Snariadne. "What's *that*?" Finn asks, as you had suspected he would.

"That's our statue of Snariadne, the Merzood spirit of chance and exploration." She has many tails and long blue hair, and sometimes, when currents flow a certain way, Snariadne glows bright blue.

Together you swim farther and farther through the city, getting closer to your destination. You swim past the reef, noting its white skeleton-like color. The current of the blue-green water carries plastic bags and other pieces of garbage. As you swim, you collect the bags to use as carriers for anything you find in the yacht. Finn tries to help, but his fins are too short. He ends up carrying a single plastic bag in his mouth.

By the time you reach the yacht, the ocean has brightened. Your Aunties should be waking up and the reef will start buzzing with activity soon. You had left them a note to let them know where you were going. In stark contrast to the bustling reef, the area where you're seeking is completely silent and empty. You swim over a patch of brain coral and spy the yacht.

Turn to page 7.

It's hanging upside down, dangerously balanced over a deep ravine and surrounded by great white sharks. Great whites are the ultimate seekers, but they always leave you alone. Sharks are not interested in eating you—they prefer seals!

You swim through a huge crack in the yacht's stern. From there, you swim into the living quarters. You look around for Strider objects, but for some reason it looks like it's already been seeked clean.

Suddenly you hear a scuttling noise. "Finn?" you call, but you don't hear a response, and the silence is ominous. You hear the drag of pincers across the floor and see a flash of green light coming from the next room. You peek through the doorway.

Two green glowing creatures scuttle around the ceiling and snap at things around the room. They have lobster faces and pincers, but they also have long green tentacles. Their mouths are filled with circular rows of tiny, sharp teeth. *These are the mutant Atlantean guards. If they're here that means the Ruler is still active!*

You cover your mouth and try to escape, but you don't think about where you're swimming. You clumsily hit a shelf on your way out. The shelf holds a huge amount of Strider food. All the cans roll down to the bow of the ship. The yacht loses its hold on the cliff. You swim through an open porthole as the yacht falls into the ravine.

Turn to page 12.

8

You rocket over the reef, and after a rough ride of twists and turns, the blindfold is ripped from your face. Your eyes adjust to the green glow of an underground cave. The cave is filled with barrels of toxic-looking green fluid. The Ruler of Atlantis sits high on a throne of discarded oysters, a creepy grin stretched across his face.

"Hello, Neruvid," the Ruler cackles. "You have been brought to the Court of High Seas as an enemy of the kingdom. Would you happen to know anything about an accident in a yacht today?" You shuffle uncomfortably. You hear a loud *thud!* in the back of the room, and the Ruler bangs his gavel. "Your family has been imprisoned in our dungeons, and you will be imprisoned with them unless you agree to help me." The Ruler waves his claw, and a large image of a glowing stone is brought before you. The stone is eye-shaped and bright blue with a dark blue center.

"This is the Eye, an Atlantean treasure that was stolen from us. Some say it was stolen by the Striders, but others believe it was lost in the Abyss. If you can find the Eye and return it to me, I will grant your and your family's freedom . . ."

Turn to page 10.

10

The Ruler stares hungrily at the poster, and green slime drips from his mouth. He leans forward so his face is right next to yours. "Beware, Neruvid, the Eye has many impersonators. There are lots of blue stones out there, but the Eye has a dark blue center, like the pupil of an *eye*! Get it?" The guards laugh and the Ruler bangs his gavel. The crowd falls silent.

"Now you must choose your place of exile: the Strider world of Brooklyn or the Abyss!" The crowd gasps. Your breath catches in your gills. The Strider world is vast, but you may be able to find your relatives in Brooklyn. On the other hand your Aunties have always said that the Abyss holds secrets of the deep, and maybe that includes the Eye?

If you choose exile to Brooklyn, go on to the next page.

If you choose exile to the Abyss, turn to page 23.

The guards blindfold you and put you back on the manta ray. As you near Rockaway Beach, a blue flash sends a forceful current of bubbles at you and the guards. The bubbles tear through the seaweed blindfold and send the guards flying backward.

The blue light shimmers into an apparition of Snariadne. She takes your hands, and you have a vision. . . .

You see a female Merzood transforming on the beach at Coney Island. Next to her is a baby swaddled in seaweed, wearing a blue ring on a chain around her neck. The moment her tail transforms into legs, she flees the beach and runs into Luna Park. A green glow slowly fills the bay and five Atlantean guards surface cautiously on their manta rays, but they're too late! The mother and baby have successfully escaped them.

In a blue flash you see a grandmother holding a baby. She rocks the baby back and forth and the baby reaches up, grabbing at her chain with a blue ring on it.

The vision disappears, and then you see a young girl sitting with her mother at Coney Island. "Rabbit, this necklace has been in our family for generations, and now that it's your thirteenth birthday, I can give it to you." Rabbit takes the necklace and puts it on.

Another blue flash and you're back with Snariadne. She claps her hands together and a small whirlpool forms. The whirlpool produces two objects: a blue crystal cylinder and a small black quartz sculpture.

To take the crystal cylinder, turn to page 13.

To take the sculpture, turn to page 19.

12

You swim back to the Hideaway as fast as you can, but when you get there, it's been ransacked and your Aunties are gone.

"Auntie Echo? Auntie Quell?" you call out.

But no one answers. Your Hideaway is filled with acid-green ink. You fan the ink with your tail and it transforms into a triangle with an eye in the center: the symbol of the Atlantean government!

An Atlantean guard scuttles down from the ceiling. "The Ruler has requested your presence. You must come with me." You feel a pair of pincers wrap around your tail, and tentacles place a pair of green glowing cuffs on your wrists.

"You have one chance to comply, or I will be forced to take precautionary measures to ensure your safe delivery to the Ruler," the guard growls.

The Atlantean guard places you on a jet-black manta ray and wraps a seaweed blindfold around your eyes. He snaps at the manta ray, and you take off for the secret Atlantean fortress.

Turn to page 8.

Snariadne disappears in a blue flash, and you're left holding the glass cylinder. You take the cylinder in your hands and turn one side until you hear it click. Then you line up the other side and turn it. *Click*. You turn both sides in opposite directions and pull them apart. The cylinder falls open. Heart racing, you pull a piece of parchment out of it. It is a map with the Brooklyn Bridge on one side and an image of the Eye on the other. The map is filled with blurry pathways and X's. . . .

You hear the furious guards returning on the manta ray. You fold up the map and hide it in your gill flap. The guards seize you, speeding to the outskirts of Coney Island.

You see a rusted, barnacle-covered sign for Coney Island's Luna Park. It has been spray-painted with the words "SAVE THE PLANET." Half-sunken amusement park rides lie dormant on what used to be Rockaway Beach.

What an awesome place to seek! you think to yourself as the manta ray zooms over the old Luna Park gates, covered in fields of kelp, and over the old boardwalk, now covered in mussels.

Turn to the next page.

The guards drop you near the new Coney Island's Luna Park, now called "Aqua Park." It was renamed after sea levels rose. When you surface at Aqua Park, you see Striders in scuba gear celebrating the Mermaid Parade on the new boardwalk.

Immediately, you spot a girl in a green mermaid outfit wearing a red backpack. You swim a little closer and see a blue ring around her neck. Could this person be Rabbit's daughter or granddaughter? She looks almost identical to the Rabbit in the vision you saw. Her family must be related to the Merzoods in some way. You wonder if they still have any Merzood powers.

Go on to the next page.

The sun disappears behind a cloud, and a chilly wind blows through the boardwalk. You swim around Rabbit's granddaughter. She looks very sad. Maybe a quest for the Eye will cheer her up? You pull yourself up onto a secluded part of the boardwalk and wait for your tail to transform into legs. You approach her, trying to figure out how to start talking to her, but the second you sit down she turns to you and between sniffles asks, "You look so familiar. Do we know each other?"

"Are you related to someone named Rabbit?" you ask.

She looks shocked. "My grandmother's name was Rabbit. But she disappeared many years ago at sea," the young girl replies. "I am named after her."

You smile.

"Nice to meet you, Rabbit. I'm Neru." Rabbit stands up and puts out her right hand. You forgot about this Strider custom. The two of you shake. "Why are you upset?" you ask.

Rabbit sniffles. "I wanted to join the Mermaid Parade, but I have a . . . condition," she replies.

"A condition?" you ask.

Turn to the next page.

Rabbit nods. "Thalassophobia. I am terrified of the ocean."

Ordinarily, you would never reveal your identity to a Strider, but Rabbit might be a Merzood!

"Just a second," you say to Rabbit. "I have something to show you." You dive off the boardwalk. Rabbit watches, fascinated and amazed, as you transform back into a Merzood. "I'll make you a deal. I can help you overcome your thalassophobia," you say. "But I need your help in return."

"What kind of help?" Rabbit asks.

"I need help finding an Atlantean treasure called the Eye," you explain. "It should be somewhere on this map."

Rabbit doesn't hesitate. "You're on!"

You climb back on land and sit down after shifting to Strider form. Rabbit pores over the treasure map while you explain about the Ruler of Atlantis kidnapping your family and exiling you to Brooklyn. She frowns in sympathy, studying the map.

"I know what to do," Rabbit says suddenly. "Follow me."

With that, you and Rabbit set off for the bridge. You catch the Scuba Sub at Ocean Parkway as it starts to rain. You and Rabbit speed through an underwater subway track to the bridge.

Turn to page 18.

18

Like it always did when it was called the Subway, the Scuba Sub gets delayed between Coney Island and the Brooklyn Bridge. The bridge used to be over a hundred feet above the water, but since the rise of the sea level, the river frequently floods it.

When you get off the Scuba Sub, the rain is pelting down and you can hear thunder rumbling. You and Rabbit walk onto the bridge and try to look at the map, but the wind rips at it. Now that you've begun the quest, the map is automatically filling itself out. There is a trail leading to the Brooklyn Bridge and a trail leading to the bottom of the bridge. The treasure is somewhere on the base of the bridge. You'll have to get in the water to find the next clue.

The water gets rougher. You try to get off the bridge before the storm really hits, but waves are already starting to flow over the walkway, blocking your exit.

"How is this supposed to improve my fear of the ocean?" Rabbit asks nervously as large waves wash over the bridge. You hold Rabbit's hand, attempting to keep your breathing calm and even. Another wave hits you both in the back. You look around for a way to get to safety. You see that you can either climb down the bridge or jump off the bridge.

If you choose to climb down the bridge, turn to page 26.

If you choose to jump off the bridge, turn to page 39.

You choose the sculpture and Snariadne disappears in a snap of bubbles. You examine the sculpture: one side of it is made of lava rock and has a carving of a smiling Merzood skeleton. The other side is made of quartz and has a carving of Snariadne. You take both sides and turn one of them so the skeleton is no longer upside down. The sculpture sends out a stream of black ink. The ink swirls for a moment and then settles into the image of a whale, but underneath the whale are Strider legs. You've never seen anything like it before.

The shadow of the Atlantean manta ray spreads over you. You hide the sculpture in your gill flap and look up. The guards, still dizzy from Snariadne's bubble explosion, seize you again and you zoom to the outskirts of Rockaway Beach. The guards drop you off near Luna Park, the old amusement park that was flooded when sea levels rose. Coney Island is still open, but it is now called "Aqua Park" and is the world's first amphibious amusement park.

Turn to the next page.

The guards remain, watching you as you swim toward Aqua Park, through rusted rides, debris, and old Strider restaurants. You surface for a moment and see hundreds of Striders gathered in the center of Aqua Park for a parade. You swim closer to check it out.

Turn to page 25.

"I choose exile to the Abyss," you say steadily. The Ruler flicks his pincer at the guards.

"As you wish, Neruvid," the Ruler snorts. The Atlantean guards replace your blindfold and whisk you away.

The next time they rip off your blindfold, you are floating above a craggy hole in the ocean floor. Sea urchins line the outside of the entrance to the long tunnel that leads to the Abyss. An Atlantean guard adds two weights to your green glowing cuffs and pushes you into the hole. You sink deeper and deeper, with only the green light of your cuffs to illuminate your descent.

Toward the bottom, you feel tiny tentacles wrapping around you. At first you try to fight them, but then you feel the cuffs and weights loosen. By the time you reach the ocean floor, the cuffs and the weights have been removed. Finding yourself plunged suddenly into darkness, you grab your cuffs before they can float away. You wave to the tiny, white-eyed creatures; they make a high-pitched sound and swim back into their tiny caves.

Turn to the next page.

24

It is so dark in the Abyss. The water is freezing and everything feels heavier; the water pressure is much more intense this deep. From your Strider encyclopedia you learned that this area of the ocean is called the Abyssopelagic Zone, and it is between 13,000 and 19,000 feet deep! You look around, using the green glow of your cuffs as a flashlight. You have been dropped into a massive sea monster skeleton. The green glow of the cuffs illuminates the huge rib cage around you. Your ears perk up, and you hear a deep-sea rhythm rising from the depths.

If you choose to follow the mysterious music, turn to page 31.

If you choose to explore the sea monster carcass, turn to page 42.

The parade is lively, and Striders dive and dance around the park. Boats decorated with glittering tentacles, sparkly scales, and fish tails idle around a purple and blue pirate ship. Striders on the pirate ship wear crowns made of coral and seaweed gowns, and dance to the music pumping out of the crow's nest speakers.

So far you don't see any clues that might help you find the Eye, but there is something that feels right about the parade.

You could join the Striders on the ship or stake out the parade from a distance.

If you choose to join the Striders on the ship, turn to page 29.

If you choose to stake out the parade from a distance, turn to page 40.

Both of you carefully make your way over the railing and down to the base of the bridge. Suddenly a rogue wave crashes against the bridge. It hits Rabbit squarely in the face and she slips, tumbling into the swirling water. You immediately dive in after her. When you reach her in the river, she is twisting and turning, sprouting a green tail and golden gills. She's transforming into a Merzood! Rabbit does a flip and swims over to you. "I'm not scared anymore! It sounds corny but I guess I just needed to dive in!"

You and Rabbit swim down to the bridge's foundation and look around for markings or secret trapdoors. Then behind some grass you notice a hole with an old carving of a sea dragon's teeth around it. The hole looks like it would fit one of your arms.

"What do you think?" you ask Rabbit.

"You helped me, so now I owe you a favor," she replies. "If you tell me to stick my arm in that hole, I'll do it."

If you choose to put your arm in the hole, turn to page 34.

If you choose to ask Rabbit to put her arm in the hole, turn to page 46.

You pull yourself up onto the ship and wait until your tail transforms into legs. When you transform, your tail turns into a scaly jumpsuit, and it fits in perfectly with the costumes at the Mermaid Parade. You jump into the crowd of dancing Striders. You get lots of compliments on your "costume"!

A Strider dressed as a jellyfish takes the stage and places a blue-cloth-covered object on a pedestal at the center of the ship. The jellyfish taps on a wireless mic and gets the crowd's attention.

"We are thrilled to see you at the 100th anniversary of Mermaid Parade!" says the jellyfish, and the crowd goes wild. "This year is extra special and so we have rescued a Mermaid Parade relic from the deep: the original Mermaid Queen crown!" The jellyfish pulls the blue cloth off to reveal the original crown.

The blue stone in the center of the crown is blindingly bright. You see the telltale dark blue pupil of the Eye. You hear the jellyfish mention something about a competition for the crown—an artistry contest and a swimming contest. You run toward the jellyfish to signal that you want to participate.

"Wow, we have an enthusiastic participant here! Which contest would you like to take part in?" Swimming seems like a natural choice, but with your skills as a seeker, you know that you could stand a good chance in the artistry competition as well.

If you choose to do the swimming competition, turn to page 99.

If you choose to compete in the artistry competition, turn to page 100.

You swim through the access door of the cave that leads to the center of the Atlantean fortress. From there, you follow the tunnel to the Throne Room. You throw open the door and enter with the glowing stone from the cave. You notice that because you're holding the stone, it has turned blue and is glowing steadily. You tell the Ruler that you will return the power source only if your demands are met. The Ruler sits back and flicks his tail fin at you.

You proceed with your demands: peace between the Atlanteans and the Merzoods. The Atlanteans must return the reef that they have been occupying and release all the prisoners from the dungeons. The Ruler laughs and the guards attempt to seize you. You dodge them and accidentally drop the power source, shattering it on the stone floor.

Your body begins to glow blue. The guards step back and drop their weapons. "Sea witch! Sea witch!" they yell. With a flick of your tail fin, you send a blue laser of light into the guards. Whatever the laser hits changes into a different creature. It's a game of chance, just like something Snariadne would do. You shoot lasers all over the room. The lobster guards look down at their new tails, tentacles, and teeth. They drop their weapons and bow down.

"We are at your service, Snariadne . . ."

The Ruler yells angrily and you turn your laser powers on him. The Ruler's robes rise and fall. There is a tiny bump moving around underneath the royal vestments. You lift the collar to find a very angry sea slug, cursing you with his tiny fins.

The End

You swim through the darkness toward the music. It leads you to a sunken tanker with a blue glow emanating from the center.

You look through the rusted side of the tanker and see a rock band practicing. A chorus of clams harmonize to bubbly rhythms, and the lead singer, a viper fish, plays a solo with her fangs on a tin-can guitar. All the band members have instruments made from garbage found in the depths of the Abyss. The lead singer spots you and motions for the band to stop playing.

"Hi, I'm Ximz! And this is my band, the Bottom-Feeders!" She invites you onto the tanker. "Ozcah, our octopus drummer, is usually here, but there's an octopus rave near the surface! Do you want to play with us?" She gestures to the drum set made of cans, dinner plates, cups, and salvaged debris.

*If you choose to rock out,
turn to the next page.*

If you choose to just watch, turn to page 115.

You swim to the stage and Ximz flips a couple of drumsticks to you. The drumsticks are made of straws and plastic utensils, all wrapped together with wire. You settle into the drum set as the other musicians tune up: the clams harmonize, Ximz tunes her tin-can guitar, the giant isopod uses their legs to strum a bass made of discarded electric cords, and many other creatures tune their homemade instruments.

"One, two, three, four!" Ximz counts you off, and as you pound the drums, the tanker shakes to the rhythm. You do an amazing solo with a fan coral flourish, smashing the dinner plate cymbals, but when you look up everyone is silent.

You think it's just your incredible solo, but then you see the floodlight of a submarine surveying the tanker. Ximz turns to the band and yells, "HIDE!" The Bottom-Feeders swim away in different directions, and Ximz motions for you to follow her.

If you choose to follow Ximz, turn to page 68.

If you choose to hide on your own, turn to page 108.

"No, I'll do it," you tell her, with more confidence than you feel. You put your arm in the hole and feel something at the end. You grab onto it, and blue sparks flow out of the hole. You pull your arm out immediately, but it doesn't look like your arm anymore; it is covered in armor with dials and buttons all over it. You play with the buttons. One shoots a net, one turns your arm into a multi-tool including a fishbone key, and another changes your arm back to normal.

Next to the hole is a locked compartment. You press the multi-tool button and use the fishbone key on the door. The key fits! You reach in and pull out a new piece of the map. When you place the new piece and the map together, they fuse into one. A new location blooms into the old parchment: the Brooklyn Navy Yard.

Go on to the next page.

When you arrive at the Brooklyn Navy Yard, you swim between an enormous aircraft carrier and a destroyer.

"Let's look at the map," you call over to Rabbit. She nods, and the two of you swim up to the surface.

"It looks like the direction we traveled between the Brooklyn Bridge and the Navy Yard has been filled in!" Rabbit says, pointing to the map. The tracks lead to a place between the two battleships. You and Rabbit swim down between them and find an old propeller. It's too heavy to move by yourselves. You look back at your new arm and see a button on the bottom that says "bubble cannon."

"What should we do?" you ask.

"Let's set the dial to max and press the bubble cannon button," Rabbit replies, and you do as she says. The arm sucks in water and then shoots it back at the propeller in a big bubble, sending it flying into the distance. Underneath is a trapdoor. Rabbit wrenches the trapdoor open and the two of you swim into it.

Turn to the next page.

36

You enter a brain coral corridor filled with mosaics. You signal to Rabbit and she follows as you swim through lots of twists and turns. "It's taking us back to the same place!" you say, frustrated. The corridor is maze-like, and you realize, "It's a brain coral labyrinth."

Rabbit looks intrigued, and you continue: "The best way to solve a labyrinth is to stay consistent. Let's keep our right hands on the wall and follow that." You and Rabbit run your hands along the wall. When you touch the mosaics, they glow brighter and the small figures peel off the walls and follow you through the maze. They even try to lead you away from the center, but despite their best efforts you arrive.

The center of the labyrinth is a glowing temple filled with electric-blue fish and bubbling urns. In the middle of the temple there is a dark blue triangular stone suspended in the air. It's not the Eye, but it looks like it could be valuable. You reach for the stone, but Rabbit grabs your arm.

"Wait," she says, "I'm not sure if you should do that . . ."

*If you choose to take the stone,
turn to page 44.*

*If you choose to ask Rabbit what you should
do, turn to page 61.*

Even though she may have a connection to your family, you don't feel like you can tell Mirra the truth.

"I, um . . . I lost a bet!" you say, inventing wildly. "My friends dared me to go into the Kelp Forest as a joke, but then I got lost."

"So you're just trespassing in the sacred forest then?" Mirra asks. You can tell this makes her angry. "I guess you were looking for the sea witch, eh?" You nod, a little unsure what she means by that.

"Let's have some tea and I'll tell you all about her," Mirra says.

She smiles and puts some potions together in a little black cup. She offers it to you, and you take a sip. Suddenly you feel your arms and legs getting slippery and long. They turn green and slightly translucent. Your tail splits into roots and your body into long leaves. You manage to let out a bubbly scream before you turn into kelp. Later that night, she plants you in the Kelp Forest.

The End

You grab Rabbit's hand and yell over the crash of the waves, "We have to jump!"

Rabbit shakes her head. "No way!" she screams. Before you can respond, another wave hits your back and drags you over the bridge and into the river.

In the churning water, you see Rabbit clinging onto the railing of the Brooklyn Bridge. She pulls herself up and gets back on the bridge. You reach out to her, but the swirling current pulls you under and takes you deeper, back to the open ocean.

A sudden rush of bubbles pulls you in. You look around and see baleen and a huge tongue. You are in the mouth of a blue whale! You follow a buzzy humming sound into the back of the whale's mouth and come face to face with a prawn. She gurgles and snaps her pincers with surprise, stunning you momentarily. You shake it off and turn back to the prawn, who apologizes. "So sorry, you startled me . . . I haven't seen anyone in a long time. I am Dr. Tocetidon, disgraced scientist and full-time dentist. What's your name?"

"I'm . . . dizzy," you say, still stunned.

"I'm sorry," she says again. "When I snap my pincers it releases bubbles that stun intruders."

When you're feeling like yourself again, you and Dr. T get to know each other. You tell her about the Eye and how the Ruler imprisoned your family. It turns out that she was once the Ruler of Atlantis's personal scientist, and she has lots to tell you.

If you choose to hear more about Dr. Tocetidon's story, turn to page 53.

If you escape the whale, turn to page 82.

40

You swim around the perimeter of the parade and check it out from there. You see a group of Striders wearing jumpsuits preparing a huge whale puppet.

You swim up alongside a puppeteer wearing goggles and she turns to you. "Are you the new fin flicker?" she asks. You look around and realize she's talking to you. Without thinking, you nod.

She sighs. "You're late. Go join the puppeteers who control the left flipper." You swim over to them.

"You must be the replacement that Blinx found," says a puppeteer with long white hair and a blue jumpsuit. "I'm Rollo, and this is Ima." Ima looks at you nervously. "Do you need us to go over the plan or did Blinx brief you? I know it's last-minute, but this is our only opportunity. I guess Blinx didn't give you a costume either. Well, you'll just blend in. Nice costume tail by the way, it looks so real!" Rollo smiles.

You nod again.

"Rollo, are you sure this is going to work?" asks Ima. "What if they notice that the fin stops moving, or what if this new person messes it up?"

"No way, Ima," Rollo grumbles, "the plan is foolproof. After the second dive the fin basically moves itself and we can sneak off to the Aquarium and steal the relic." Rollo looks at you. "Blinx explained this, right? Are you ready for the heist?"

If you choose to go along with the heist, turn to page 86.

If you choose to refuse the heist, turn to page 88.

You decide that releasing the eels is too risky. If the Atlantean guards catch you helping the eels, they will destroy any hope you have of saving your Aunties. You swim away from the eels and back toward Merzood City.

You hear the rush of manta rays above you. The water fills with an eerie green glow. You can hear the snap of pincers. The Atlantean guards surround you and put a pair of heavy green cuffs on you. They take you back to the Atlantean fortress, but they don't lock you in the dungeon with your Aunties. Instead, you are forced to work at the manta ray stable. Every day, all day, you clean up manta ray poop and fill the feeding pit with plankton. You think about your Aunties constantly, but the guards keep a close eye on you, and escaping the stable is impossible.

The End

The strange music could be a trap set by the Atlantean guards! You decide to explore the sea monster carcass instead of following the music. You swim into the monster's huge jaws, and then your light catches on something shiny caught in the monster's huge teeth.

You yank it out and dust it off. It looks exactly like the suits that Striders used to wear to explore the ocean. It has a circular helmet with a few portholes and a protective body suit. You pat the side of the suit and feel something hard in the lining. You rip it open and find a glass cylinder. You open it and unfurl an old piece of parchment.

A mysterious light appears in the distance, and it makes the parchment even easier to read. There are little trails leading to inky areas and faded X's all over the place. *This must be an old Strider treasure map*, you think. You turn it over and in the center of the page is a stone that looks just like the Eye!

Your heart starts pounding. Though the map is faded in some parts, the first stop is still readable. It seems to be underneath the Brooklyn Bridge. There must be a tidal current you can take to get to Brooklyn. You look around for any creatures you could ask, and that's when you notice that the mysterious light has been getting steadily closer to you.

"Hello?" you ask, but no one answers.

If you choose to swim away from the mysterious light, turn to page 49.

If you choose to investigate the mysterious light, turn to page 55.

You wait until your past self chooses the exile in the Abyss. The guards hustle you out and blindfold you again. They put your past self back on a manta ray, but just as the manta is about to take off, you slide underneath it and hang on tight. You recall that the ride to the Abyss was long and treacherous, but it's worse underneath the manta ray. You have to hold on tight to avoid getting knocked off by the sharp rocks, dips, and turns. The moment you enter a straightaway, you climb onto the manta's back to attempt to pull the guards away from the driver's seat.

Just moments into the tussle, the guards duck. You see, dead ahead, a low arch of sea-urchin-covered rock. You try to duck, but it's too late and you slam into the arch. You sink down into the deep, unable to save your past self from the Abyss.

The End

44

You decide not to listen to Rabbit and take the stone. The moment you pluck the stone from its resting place, the blue fish start to swarm you. A shrill scream rises from the depths, and you hear something huge shifting underneath the labyrinth. The floor below starts to splinter and crack.

"I told you not to take the stone!" Rabbit yells. You and Rabbit swim into the labyrinth, which begins to collapse around you. Brain coral rubble falls, trapping you in a cage of coral. Two blue eyes filled with bubbling flames appear in the darkness. The last thing you see is the sea dragon's jaws open, producing a twirling spire of blue flaming bubbles.

The End

You decide to make a disturbance and push over some of the barrels of green glowing sludge. The green sludge fills the room, and the water gets murky. You swim over to yourself and whisper in your ear: "The Eye is in Brooklyn." Then you disappear into the murky green glow. The Ruler bangs the gavel and the guards roughly reestablish order. You swim into the shadowy passageway and listen for your decision. You hear yourself choose exile to Brooklyn. Suddenly the device chirps and blurps, and the sea cave disappears into the tunnel of bubbles.

BANG! You merge with your own body in a blue flash of light. You look around. You are in a blue open space, but soon the Atlantean guards catch up with you. They pull you back onto the manta ray and speed to your destination. You zoom over Luna Park, the amusement park that was abandoned when sea levels rose. Schools of fish swim through tattered tents, rusted rides, and signs spray-painted with phrases like **SAVE OUR OCEANS!** and **BE GREEN!** The guards drop you off on the outskirts of the new water park called "Aqua Park."

When you surface at Aqua Park, you see Striders in scuba gear celebrating the 100th anniversary of the Mermaid Parade on the boardwalk. You spot a girl in a green mermaid outfit wearing a red backpack. When you swim even closer you see a blue ring around her neck. She looks almost identical to the Rabbit you saw in your vision. It seems like this person could be Rabbit's daughter or granddaughter!

Turn to page 15.

46

Rabbit shuts her eyes and slowly extends her arm into the hole. After a tense moment, there's a slithering sound and blue ink flows out of the hole. Immediately, Rabbit pulls her arm out, but it has been transformed into a tentacle! Rabbit wiggles her new appendage and releases some ink. The ink drifts over the map and fills in a faded section.

A new portion of the map appears: a grassy hill covered in headstones and an obelisk. "That's the Tomb of Secrets in Green-Wood Cemetery," Rabbit says excitedly. You and Rabbit surface and get back on the Scuba Sub. As your tails transform to legs and feet, you both notice that Rabbit's tentacle arm is also changing back to its original form. By the time the Scuba Sub arrives, the weather has cleared.

The Scuba Sub splashes through Brooklyn. Brownstones and old city streets swirl by as you speed toward Sunset Park. The Scuba Sub car is filled with commuters and families wearing snorkels and goggles. You and Rabbit hang on as the Sub purrs like a cuttlefish through the underwater system. You exit the Scuba Sub at 25th Street and walk the few blocks to Green-Wood Cemetery.

You and Rabbit hike through the muddy cemetery. You trip on a root and rip the map as you fall. You shake off the mud and check the map. The map has ripped along perforated lines. This part of the map is meant to be removed! You tear off the small rectangular portion of the map and slowly the words "Admit One" appear.

Turn to page 48.

48

You arrive at the Tomb of Secrets, a large marble obelisk that reads: "Here lie the secrets of the visitors of Green-Wood Cemetery." The obelisk has a rectangular slit for pieces of paper, and you slip the ticket in. You wait a few seconds and feel the ground shift underneath you.

A trapdoor opens underneath you, and you both fall into an underground chamber. You and Rabbit land in a hollowed-out log meant for one. A river flows beneath you. Suddenly a bell rings and the log drifts forward, picking up speed. The two of you zoom down a narrow passageway. The log flume takes you through an underground passage across Brooklyn, through catacombs and abandoned subway stations. You reach the top of an underground mountain and the log tips forward, speeding through the darkness. You and Rabbit splash into a storm drain. You get off the log flume and the current pulls it back, generating blue sparks as it climbs.

You are in the abandoned part of Luna Park, back in Coney Island. You and Rabbit surface and look around. You see the Cyclone and the Wonder Wheel a few fin flicks away. You look at the map, and the park is beginning to fill in. You see the Wonder Wheel and the now-abandoned Luna Park.

If you choose to explore the rest of the abandoned part of the park, turn to page 56.

If you choose to go on the Wonder Wheel, turn to page 65.

Something, perhaps a sea sense, tells you to swim away from the light. You roll up the map and swim away from the sea monster carcass. Suddenly, you bump into something rubbery.

"Hello?" a sing-song voice says in the darkness. You shine your light around, and accidentally straight into the enormous eye of a giant squid! You swim back in fright.

"Don't be afraid!" the giant squid says. She holds out a tentacle for you to sit on. "My name is Veloras. I saw you swim away from that light. That was a smart move; that anglerfish is always hungry about now." Veloras tells you that anglerfish use their bioluminescent lights to attract prey.

You ask Veloras whether there's a way to get out of the Abyss fast and undetected. She tells you about the Drain, a secret commuter tidal current used by all the creatures who live in the Abyss. She says that it will get you out of the Abyss, but she warns you that it moves fast. You could miss your stop and end up following the Gulf Stream all the way up the coast.

If you choose to follow Veloras to the Drain, turn to the next page.

If you choose to find your own way, turn to page 71.

50

The Drain sounds like a perfect way to evade the guards and get back to the Hideaway. You can handle the speed of the current; you're a Merzood! You tell Veloras that you want to go to the Drain, and she places you gently on her mantle and whisks you away to the entrance of the Drain.

After you arrive at the entrance, you wait in line behind other creatures. Veloras instructs you to get off as soon as the water gets lighter. When it's your turn, you suddenly feel a pang of anxiety, but when a clear spot appears, Veloras pushes you forward.

Go on to the next page.

You jump into the Drain and get pulled along by the relentless tidal current. Creatures rush by you at warp speed. They are all commuting to different reefs and beyond.

"Excuse me, how do I exit the Drain?" you ask a passing sea turtle.

"Just stand on my shell and jump off," he says. You barely grab on as he slows slightly. You see the current bend, and then the water lightens. You try to jump out of the current, but a plume of bubbles pushes you past your home reef and you miss your stop. Oh well. . . .

The next stop is Coney Island. This time the sea turtle pushes you, and you flip out of the Drain. In front of you is the old Coney Island boardwalk, which was used years ago before the sea levels rose. You swim by a barnacle-covered sign that says **WORLD FAMOUS LUNA PARK!** The sign is now rusted, with all kinds of fish swimming around it. Coney Island went under when sea levels rose, but came back when Aqua Park, the world's first amphibious theme park, was opened.

You catch your breath, and you surface briefly. You see signs for the 100th anniversary of the Mermaid Parade. Striders wearing scuba gear, mermaid tails, and lobster claws explore the park. The water is filled with decorated boats and floats. In the center of Aqua Park is a blue and purple pirate ship. You swim toward it.

Turn to page 29.

Dr. Tocetidon tells you that the Eye is one of many energy crystals that contain the ocean's light, but it happens to be especially large and powerful. "There are lots of fakes and many smaller crystals, but you'll know it's the Eye because it will have a dark blue stone inside the center . . ." The whale burps.

She continues, "If the Ruler gets the Eye it will spell doom for so many creatures. The Ruler will make light scarce and sell it only to the highest bidder. Light, a necessity, will benefit only those few who can afford the Ruler's prices. That doesn't seem fair, does it? Light should be free for everyone! It's a basic right for every creature in the ocean!

"I have enough evidence to take action against the Ruler," Dr. T tells you. "But I need someone who is dedicated to the cause to assist me."

You have never even considered taking action against the Ruler until now, and the prospect is exciting.

Turn to the next page.

You think about Rabbit and feel a deep pang of regret. You wish you could have helped her more with her fear of the ocean, but your Aunties need you.

You decide to stay in the whale and become Dr. T's assistant.

"What we need to do," Dr. T explains, "is develop an extensive case on the corrupt Ruler of Atlantis and take it straight to the Court of High Seas."

"Let's get to work!" you reply.

You spend weeks on your case, and finally the Ruler is found guilty and stripped of power, and your family goes free.

You and Dr. T are heralded as heroes for stopping the Ruler's evil plan and for making the ocean a better place for all creatures, not just the ones who have lots of power.

The End

You swim hesitantly toward the light to contact whoever it's attached to. Small fish swim around the dazzling white light. Suddenly a tranquil feeling flows over you. This must be a light to help lost souls in the Abyss. . . .

"Hello?" you whisper again.

"Well, if it isn't lunch . . ." A gleeful voice laughs in the darkness. A crescent-shaped jaw full of jagged teeth closes over you. The anglerfish swallows you. Everything fades to black.

The End

56

You and Rabbit decide to explore the abandoned part of the park. You swim deeper until you reach the original Coney Island boardwalk and search for signs or clues that might lead to the Eye. You swim by the old Tea Party ride, the blue and white teacups now broken, home to mussels and clams. You swim around the loops of the Thunderbolt, and a school of electric-blue fish joins you.

You follow the school of fish as they swim deeper into the abandoned park. The rides are getting more rusted, and piles of debris get higher. Suddenly, a blue flash catches your eye. For a moment you see something that looks like a Merzood, but it disappears into the cracked foundation of the aquarium. You and Rabbit pump your tails and follow. A blue glow starts to change the water around you. It feels warmer and lighter.

Go on to the next page.

You and Rabbit swim through the ruins of the old aquarium. Schools of fish swim in and out of the exhibits. Every so often you hear voices, and you swim a little faster. You are struck by the feeling that you are returning home. The voices echo through the currents that flow around you.

Ahead of you is a huge crack in the foundation of the aquarium. You swim into it and listen; the voices are getting louder. The glow brightens and you swim into a secret sea cave in the foundation of the aquarium.

Turn to the next page.

58

When you enter the sea cave, you see what appears to be a group of Merzoods. You look around, gaping at them.

"Hello, my name is Mina. What's yours?" says the one you perceive to be the leader. She has a sword for an arm and a brilliant green and yellow tail.

Go on to the next page.

"I'm Neruvid, but you can call me Neru. This is Rabbit," you say. "What is this place?"

"This is our rebel hideout. We call ourselves the Zombie Zoos," Mina says, and a few others chuckle. "We may be exiled, but we still maintain the Merzood way of life. We've been in exile since before the fall of Atlantis."

You catch Mina and her clan up on what has been happening since their exile: how the Ruler kidnapped your family, and your quest to find the Eye. The Zombie Zoos are shocked when you tell them that after the fall there was a period of peace, but now the Ruler is attacking the Merzoods again.

"If the Ruler is gathering power, we must stop him before he takes over again!" Mina says. You and Rabbit agree, and together with the Zombie Zoos you develop a plan for a daring rescue and redistribution of the Ruler's power.

Turn to the next page.

Sometime later, after information gathering and numerous stakeouts, you and the Zombie Zoos attack the Atlantean fortress. According to your intel, the Atlantean fortress is powered by electric eels. You and the Zombie Zoos sneak into the power station and release the eels. The sudden blackout causes the fortress to fall into chaos. During the chaos, Mina and the Zombie Zoos take the Ruler hostage.

You and Rabbit swim straight to the dungeon to rescue your Aunties. When you released the eels, the electrified dungeon doors opened and allowed all the prisoners to escape. You bump into your Aunties on the way to the dungeons.

"Auntie Quell! Auntie Echo!" you cry when you spot them. The three of you join in a huge hug.

"The Zombie Zoos helped us storm the fortress," you explain.

Auntie Echo interrupts, saying, "I have an idea. Can you take us to the Throne Room?"

You and Rabbit nod. "Follow us," Rabbit says.

The four of you swim in a rush to the Throne Room. Several members of the Zombie Zoo clan follow. Once there, your Aunties and the Zombie Zoos join hands and create a huge bubble portal that transports the Atlantean fortress and the kingdom to the center of Brooklyn's sewer system.

After the second fall of Atlantis, Mina is named the Facilitator of the Merzood community, and a new era of Merzood history begins.

The End

"What should we do, Rabbit?" you ask.

Rabbit is studying the mosaics. She runs her hand over the walls and the figures jump out of their grooves, eager to show her the stories within. The blue figures and Merzood symbols swirl around you. Rabbit looks at them closely, describing what she sees.

"There are symbols to paint, rites to repeat, and there's something else here too . . . an ancient power or a creature? It's a summoning ritual, but I'm not sure what it summons." You both look at the stone in the center of the temple. It is very tooth-like.

Rabbit reaches into the bubbling urns and uses the glowing liquid to draw triangles around your eyes and mouth and on the palms of your hands. She paints a triangle on the floor to protect where you're both standing. You join hands around the bowl. "Close your eyes and hum," Rabbit tells you, and you start to harmonize with her.

The floor shifts underneath you. The brain coral starts to crumble and fall away, except for the space where Rabbit drew the triangle. The fallen stones reveal a deep chasm, so dark it might be endless.

Turn to the next page.

Something shifts in the murky chasm and two blazing blue eyes beam through the darkness. The eyes get larger as they get closer, and the sea dragon's cold breath makes you shiver. You and Rabbit look at each other, shocked.

"Okay, you can stop humming now . . . you summoned me, what do you want?" the sea dragon grumbles in a whiny voice. When she yawns, you notice that some fangs are missing.

"Is this your tooth?" you ask, and the sea dragon nods.

"It's a trap I've set for intruders. If they grab my tooth I attack! But it's okay, I've been losing lots of teeth because my adult fangs are coming in. Clever, huh?" You and Rabbit exchange looks. You can't believe the sea dragon is going to get even bigger!

"So, we can ask you for anything?" you inquire. The sea dragon nods. "We are on a quest to find the Eye, a bright blue stone with a dark blue center," you say.

"Or you could help us overthrow the Atlantean empire," Rabbit adds.

The sea dragon thinks for a moment. "No one has ever given me a choice before. How do I decide?" she asks nervously, and looks at both of you. "I don't know what to do! I can't choose!" She starts to growl and vibrate. You and Rabbit try to get her to calm down, but she roars and dives back into the depths.

Suddenly you hear a huge explosion erupt from the depths, and the brain coral labyrinth rocks. Silvery blue fins float up, and a blue glow emanates from the darkness.

Go on to the next page.

You and Rabbit dive into the darkness and swim toward the blue glow. It illuminates a new sea creature, a Leviathan with huge glowing eyes and an eye-shaped mouth filled with rows of glowing teeth. It has a long translucent snake-like body with a glowing skeleton. Long bioluminescent tentacles and millions of tiny tendrils reach out to you. Rainbow lights travel up and down the Leviathan's body.

"The choice you gave me caused me to change into my final form," the Leviathan says as she throws her head back. She roars a high-pitched scream and the glow in her center materializes into a bright blue stone with a dark center. Using her tentacles, she plucks the stone from the center of her skeleton and offers it to you.

"Is that . . . ?" Rabbit murmurs.

"This is the Eye," the Leviathan says. You take the Eye, and the Leviathan's body glows brighter and brighter, the rainbow tendrils dancing as you and Rabbit leave the depths.

You and Rabbit return to Atlantis.

Turn to the next page.

"Here is the Eye!" you announce to the Ruler as you storm into the fortress. You toss the Eye across the room and he snaps it up with his claw, inspecting it closely.

"Well, well," he says, clearly impressed. "I didn't think you had it in you, little Neruvid. Guards! Release this Merzood's two relatives!"

You can hardly believe it. You and Rabbit stand frozen to the spot, afraid to move in case he changes his mind. Instead, he turns and sweeps out of the hall with the Eye, and moments later your Aunties are rushing to your side.

"Auntie Quell, Auntie Echo!" you exclaim as they hug you tight. "This is my new friend, Rabbit!"

Your Aunties stare at Rabbit in awe. "I know you," Auntie Echo says. "Or at least, I knew someone like you, many years ago . . ."

"Did you know my grandmother?" Rabbit says quietly. "She was named Rabbit too."

Your Aunties exchange a look of amazement. "Of course, you're Rabbit's granddaughter! Not only did we know her—we're related to her! You're a direct descendent of Merzoods on your mother's side." Rabbit's eyes go wide, taking this in.

"Come on," you finally say. "Let's return to the Hideaway for a well-deserved celebration!"

The End

"Let's go higher, where we'll get a better view," Rabbit says. You nod at your little friend in agreement. You swim to the base of the Wonder Wheel and dive into a green car as it dips beneath the surface. When you reach the top of the Wonder Wheel, it grinds to a halt. Now you have a view of the entire park.

"Look at that!" Rabbit squeals. The sun has finally emerged from behind the clouds, and the rays catch something brilliant and blue in the center of the parade. Could it be the Eye?

*If you choose to infiltrate the parade,
turn to the next page.*

*If you choose to consult the map,
turn to page 76.*

You and Rabbit decide to infiltrate the parade. You swim toward the purple and blue pirate ship at the center of Aqua Park.

A Strider dressed as a jellyfish is making an announcement. "We are thrilled to crown this year's Mermaid Queen! Madame Decopada!" The crowd goes wild. Madame Decopada, dressed as an elegant lobster with huge crystal pincers and orange flaming hair, steps forward and bows to the crowd. The jellyfish uncovers the Mermaid Queen crown. You see a blinding flash of blue and the dark blue pupil of the Eye. You signal to Rabbit, and the two of you dive below the crowd.

"That's the Eye!" you say excitedly. "And I have a plan to get it."

Go on to the next page.

Your plan involves a couple of animal friends.

You dive back under the water and clear your throat. "Hey!" you yell into the deep, using your best whale call. "I need some help!"

A humpback whale, her calf, and an octopus swim up from the bottom of the park. You huddle together and tell everyone your plan. When everyone is ready, you swim toward the pirate ship in the center of the parade.

Rabbit hides by the stage. The humpback whales dive deep and take their place beneath the pirate ship. The octopus waits underneath the crowd. You climb up on the pirate ship and transform, blending in with the Striders on the ship. When the humpback whales knock the pirate ship, you sneak up behind Madame Decopada. The octopus inks the water so no one can see anything. You bump Madame Decopada, causing the crown to fall into the murky water. You and Rabbit dive in after it. The glow of the Eye makes it easy to find in the inky darkness.

"RETREAT!" you yell to the humpbacks and the octopus. By the time Madame Decopada and the others start trying to find the crown, you and Rabbit are already riding back to the reef on the humpback whale, with the Eye safely tucked under your arm.

The End

68

You follow Ximz and the bass player out of the tanker and into a sea cave. You swim through the winding passageway. The sea cave opens right near the entrance to the Abyss. You and the band explore the sea monster carcass until it's safe to return to the tanker.

The three of you swim through the monster from end to end. You and Ximz explore the monster's huge jaws and rows of long triangular teeth. You pan your light over the mouth and something shiny catches your eye.

You swim over to it and yank the shiny object out of the teeth. It's much heavier than you imagined. You hold it up and use your light to figure out what it is. You immediately recognize it from the Strider encyclopedia you've been reading.

Turn to page 70.

It's an old diver's suit! You shake off the muck and sand. The suit has a circular metallic helmet with a few portholes for the Strider to look around. It also has a protective suit and a vest that was once attached to a cord that delivered oxygen and kept the diver close to the ship. It seems like the sea monster just swam by and snatched the diver off the ocean floor.

You pat the side of the suit and feel something hard in the lining. You rip it open and find a glass cylinder. You open the cylinder and discover an old piece of parchment.

You unroll it and find a soggy map. Blurred lines and X's crisscross the map. You turn it over, and on the back is an image of the Eye. Your breath catches in your gills. The only other part of the map that is filled in is the Brooklyn Bridge. Could this be the first stop to finding the Eye? You look around for someone to show the map to, but then wonder if you should show it to anyone.

*If you choose to show Ximz the map,
turn to page 78.*

*If you choose to keep the map to yourself,
turn to page 79.*

"That sounds too risky," you tell Veloras. "I don't want to get caught in the Gulf Stream. But thank you for your help."

You swim away, resolving to find a different way to escape the Abyss.

You swim through the darkness with the green glow lighting your way. Suddenly you bump into something hard. This time it doesn't feel like a giant squid.

You shine your light over a huge statue of Snariadne. She's covered in garbage and Abyss detritus. You can hear your Auntie Echo and your Auntie Quell groaning about how bad the shrine looks, and you feel an urge to clean it up. Maybe you should do it for your Aunties?

If you choose to clean up the Snariadne shrine,
turn to the next page.

If you choose not to clean up the shrine,
turn to page 97.

You set your broken cuffs down so you can pick up the trash around the shrine and tidy up all the sea debris. You sweep the kelp away from the rocks at the base of the statue and clean off Snariadne's face.

For a moment her eyes flash a brilliant blue. Usually, Snariadne wears a seaweed crown, and after searching, you find it a few feet away from her. You grab the crown and press it into the small holes in the statue's head. When the crown clicks back in, it opens a secret compartment in her chest. A sea slug pops out and flips with excitement. It's blue and sparkling, like a gem.

"You released me from my prison! Thank you, new friend. My name is Mika!" Mika the sea slug dances around you. "Is there anything I can do to repay this kindness?"

"Um . . . there is, actually," you say. "I'm seeking an ancient Atlantean treasure called the Eye. The Ruler of Atlantis has trapped my family in the dungeons and without this treasure he will never set them free!"

"Trapped in a dungeon, you say? I understand what that's like. Of course I'll help you."

Turn to page 74.

"We should go to Zyzi, the Trench Magician," Mika squeaks in a high-pitched voice. You and Mika swim back toward the sea monster carcass and into a cave in the walls of the Abyss.

Zyzi's cave has a pink glow to it. Mika calls his name, and you hear a crash from the back of the cave. Zyzi, a red jellyfish with a translucent top and thousands of tiny tentacles, glitters into the pink light. Zyzi and Mika swim around each other.

Go on to the next page.

"YOU!" Zyzi growls. "How dare you show your face here!"

You watch in horror as Zyzi attacks Mika, stinging him with his tendrils.

"Wait, please stop!" you scream, and Zyzi stops stinging Mika.

"My friend needs a favor, Zyzi, and then we can settle our debt," Mika squeaks weakly. Mika curls up on a sea sponge while you and Zyzi talk.

"I'm looking for the Eye," you tell Zyzi. "An old Atlantean treasure."

"I know the Eye," he replies. "And I can help you, but I need something in return."

He looks at Mika, who is now fast asleep. Zyzi tells you in a hushed voice that Mika is not a sea slug, but the spirit of a dangerous sea monster. Zyzi needs to capture him in this tiny form because his true form could bring destruction to the Abyss.

"Now that you've let Mika escape, you must help me capture him again," Zyzi tells you.

If you choose to help Zyzi capture Mika, turn to page 92.

If you choose to fight Zyzi, turn to page 113.

"Let's consult the map," you say, and Rabbit agrees. You follow the trails you've already used and look for any new clues. The drawing of the ruler Wonder Wheel has two different trails leading from it: one leads somewhere very inky and dark, and the other leads back to the abandoned part of the aquarium.

"I think we should swim back to the abandoned part of the park," you say.

"Me too!" Rabbit says.

When the Wonder Wheel dips back into the water, you and Rabbit jump off and swim on your way. You check the map again and a new place has appeared. It looks like a tunnel with sharp teeth around it, and around the teeth swim Merzoods. The image looks like it might be from an old ride.

You and Rabbit swim through the old, rusting rides and deeper into the abandoned park. A school of electric-blue fish swims past you and deeper into the park. Rabbit points to a crumbling building ahead of you. It is the old aquarium.

Suddenly, you spot a blue glow coming from the old rides. Rabbit taps you on the shoulder. "Look, there's a blue glow coming from the aquarium!" But you don't see anything. You recall what the Ruler said about the Eye having many impersonators. You must be getting closer.

If you choose to follow Rabbit to the abandoned aquarium, go on to the next page.

If you choose to explore the old rides, turn to page 83.

You and Rabbit swim toward the abandoned aquarium and enter through a huge crack in the foundation. You swim through the old exhibits. It's creepy to be in an aquarium. One of your worst fears is to be stuck in one!

You swim through empty and overgrown exhibitions, giant clams, and kelp forests, and even see some sharks scavenging for food.

Rabbit takes the lead and swims ahead. "The blue glow is getting brighter!" she calls. You still don't see anything, but you follow, checking the map to see if any new areas have appeared. It looks like the ink is changing and shifting, as if it is picking up energy that you can't feel or see.

A flash of blue interrupts your thoughts and Rabbit screams. You see the outline of a Merzood rushing deeper into the aquarium.

"Wait!" Rabbit yells, and you follow her through another crack in the foundation of the aquarium. But instead of going back into the park, you find yourself swimming into a sea cave.

Turn to page 58.

You swim back to where you thought Ximz was, but you can't find her anywhere. Frustrated, you rest on a soft spot between some craggy rocks. You shine your green light onto the map and survey it. The map is filled with differing paths and loops. Some lead to places where the ink has blurred. With your finger, you trace the different pathways to the blurry X's.

Suddenly, you feel the soft surface shift beneath you. You scan the area with your green light and see a huge eye open, then narrow in anger. Before you can escape, the enormous jaws of a giant squid wrap around you, swallowing you and the map.

The End

You tuck the map into your gill fold and set off, hoping the Bottom-Feeders don't notice you leaving. You swim back to where you entered the Abyss and peek out around the top to see if the guards are still there. Immediately the guards spot you and strike, but you act fast and swim back down.

How am I going to find the Eye if I can't get out of the Abyss? you think to yourself. You find a little place among a pile of sea monster bones and take a few breaths. You try to break the problem up into smaller parts, but that doesn't work either. Eventually you get so frustrated that you scream a stream of bubbles into the darkness.

"Hello!" says a small voice just beyond you. Suddenly a huge crescent-shaped jaw appears in front of you, and you scream, dropping your cuff-flashlight in surprise. Your scream scares the creature with the terrifying jaws and it screams too!

"I'm not going to eat you!" says the anglerfish. "My name is Wezzi, what's yours?"

"I'm Neru," you say and try to smile at Wezzi. She smiles too, but it's terrifying! "I am trying to find a way out of the Abyss besides the way I came in, but I can't find another way."

"Have you heard of the Drain? You can use that to get back to wherever you're going . . ."

"I want to go back to Merzood City." Wezzi looks perplexed. She says she's never been out of the Abyss before but offers to show you the Drain. You agree and swim next to her, using her bioluminescent light as a guide.

Turn to the next page.

80

Wezzi shows you the Drain: it's a secret opening to a tidal current that creatures use like a subway to get from one place to another. It moves so fast that the guards won't see you flying by.

"Thank you, Wezzi!" you say. You get in line for the Drain and jump in when it's your turn. The current whisks you out of the Abyss and you zoom back to Merzood City.

The Drain spits you out on the edge of the reef and you sneak back to your Hideaway. The Hideaway has been ransacked but there are no guards. All your family's art is destroyed. You sort through the debris and straighten a painting on the wall. When you turn the painting, you hear a click. On the other side of the wall, a secret door creaks open. You swim over and peer in. It's some kind of hidden compartment.

Go on to the next page.

You find two devices wrapped in dried fan coral. This must be your family's secret cache of inventions! You swim most of the way into the compartment for a closer look. One of the inventions has a blue glow, and the other emits a steady stream of purple sparks.

Suddenly you hear the sound of pincers and scuttling feet outside the door. The Atlantean guards are about to reenter the Hideaway. If they see you, you'll be at their mercy, unless you have a way to fight back. You look at the inventions again. Which one could help you escape the guards?

If you choose the invention with the blue glow, turn to page 89.

If you choose the invention with the purple sparks, turn to page 103.

"I'm sorry," you say to Dr. Tocetidon, "but I have to get back to the Brooklyn Bridge."

"I understand," she replies. "The best way out of here is through the blowhole. Good luck."

You say goodbye and crawl further into the whale's throat, but you only make it as far as the tonsils.

From the back of the throat, you see a blue glow. You crawl toward it and find a trove of stones that look similar to the Eye. Maybe you could take a few to the Ruler and he wouldn't know the difference? You pick up the biggest one you can find and make your way to the blowhole.

"Give that back!" someone screams. "I must protect it!" You look down and see a horseshoe crab with glowing blue eyes. You ask the crab their name, but they don't remember anymore. The crab doesn't remember what part of the reef they are from either, it could be anywhere. "I have to stay here and be the keeper of the EYES . . ."

The horseshoe crab turns around, and you look for a smaller stone to take. There are so many good options. You fill your arms with stones. Every time one falls out of your arms, you grab another . . . and another. . . .

You catch a glimpse of yourself in a pool of whale saliva. Your eyes are glowing, pulsing bright blue like the Eye. You spend eternity trying to collect the perfect Eye to save your family.

The End

"There has to be something more to these old rides," you say. "I'm convinced of it."

Rabbit sighs, looking wistfully at the old aquarium. "I suppose you're right. Let's go."

You swim toward the glow, passing the electric-blue fish. You take out the map and watch your trail fill in as you swim. You are getting closer to the mysterious ride.

Suddenly you're right on top of it. You and Rabbit look around, but you don't see any rides. The electric-blue fish swim into a pile of debris next to you. When you get closer you can feel a current of cold water coming through the debris. You and Rabbit move the debris and find a sign for a roller coaster called the "Mystical Mermaid." The ride is in perfect condition. The roller coaster car is ready for thrill seekers. The control panels are untouched, and the tracks are clear. Seems like with some tinkering, the Mystical Mermaid may swim again. . . .

If you choose to get the ride to work, and jump on, turn to page 85.

If you choose not to tinker with the ride, turn to page 96.

You open the control panel and look at it: it's way too waterlogged to work. The Mystical Mermaid starts on a straightaway but then it drops. You grab some wreckage and rocks to weigh the first car down. You and Rabbit push the car until the drop and jump in, speeding over the tracks. The weighted first car pulls you through the loops and hills that mimic the movement of the ocean. The walls are covered in murals of mermaids and seals dancing together in the deep. Eventually, the ride slows down on a straightaway and stops just before the scariest part.

Ahead of you is a set piece that looks like the mouth of a sea dragon, a creature with flaming blue eyes. If the ride worked, you would fly into its mouth! It looks exactly like the ink image of the sea monster on the map. The tunnel through its mouth looks dark and spooky, but it could lead to something. . . .

"What will it be?" Rabbit asks you. "Do we explore the ride or go back to the parade?"

If you choose to keep exploring the ride, turn to page 94.

If you choose to go back to the parade instead, turn to page 98.

You decide to go along with the heist.

"Here's the plan," Rollo tells you. "We're going to steal an ancient Snariadne relic."

Your heart leaps. Could that be the Eye? Rollo has intel that places the relic in Coney Island's abandoned aquarium and in the mouth of a giant clam.

You, Rollo, and Ima take your positions as the show begins. The whale enters and does its first big dive. On the second dive, the three of you drop the fin when the whale dives deeper. The momentum of the other puppeteers keeps the fin moving. You dive deep into the abandoned park and swim through a crack in the foundation. Rollo and Ima are very impressed by how long you can hold your breath. Sometimes you have to pretend you're going up for air or they'll get suspicious.

You swim through the old exhibits until you arrive at the giant clams. Ima signals that the coast guard is entering the exhibit. The three of you dash behind some kelp. Eventually, the guards pass by and into another part of the aquarium.

Rollo quietly takes his tools out of his jumpsuit and approaches the glass that surrounds the giant clam exhibition. He places a rubber suction cup on the side of the glass and attaches a wire with a shining blade. He extends the wire and quickly slices a large circle in the glass. He uses the suction cup as an anchor to pull the glass away.

Go on to the next page.

"Okay, kid, now it's your turn, go open that giant clam . . ." You gulp. "The big one that's farthest back in the tank." You hate giant clams, but you're in too deep now. You swim through the hole and up to the giant clam. The clam has been in here so long it looks almost dead, but you know better.

You give the giant clam a tickle underneath her chin. She giggles and opens her mouth for a moment. You stick a rock in the corner of her mouth and look inside.

The clam's mouth is empty. There's no relic, but the indentation from where it used to be looks just like the sculpture that Snariadne gave you. You remove the stone from the giant clam's lip. She growls angrily at you and then falls back asleep.

"Look what I found," you say, handing the sculpture over to Rollo and Ima. Rollo excitedly turns the two sides in a special pattern, and then presses into the skeleton's smile. A plume of black ink shoots out of the sculpture. Rollo and Ima scream, and for a moment you see two piercing blue eyes staring at you in the darkness.

Then the ink dissipates and all is well again. You ask Rollo what the relic does, and he says that it can predict how you will die.

The End

88

You refuse to help Rollo and Ima with their heist, but instead offer them the relic that Snariadne gave you. Rollo and Ima look shocked when you hand it to them.

"But that's it! That's the ancient Snariadne relic! I told you the legends were true!" Rollo takes the relic carefully in his hands and turns it over.

"Let me see it!" Ima grabs it. Then Rollo grabs it back and Ima takes it again. The two thieves start fighting over the relic, and it slips out of their hands. The relic sinks to the bottom of the park. Rollo and Ima rush down into the deep, never to be heard from again.

The End

The invention with the blue glow reminds you of your Aunties—all three of you wear blue rings on your fingers that have the same electric glow. You unwrap the invention and find a palm-sized circular device with holes all around it. The device has a big blue button in the center. You look for markings or instructions that might tell you what the device does, but all it says on the back is: DON'T PRESS THE BUTTON!!

The Atlantean guards burst into the Hideaway, tridents at the ready.

If you choose to press the blue button,
turn to the next page.

If you choose not to press the blue button,
turn to page 116.

The guards surround you and aim their electrified tridents at you. You press the blue button on the invention but nothing happens. You press it again and again, but nothing happens! The guards seize the invention and stamp it into the sandy ground. A few seconds later you hear a whirring, vibrating sound. . . .

The trampled invention starts to spin, levitating in the center of the room. The guards turn and watch a blue, oily liquid stream out of the holes on the side. The device beeps three times and releases hundreds of bubble portals!

The bubble portals release an avalanche of creatures. You attempt to make your escape, dodging spiked tentacles, prehistoric pincers, and gnashing teeth. A huge megalodon swims through the portal into your world. It sees you and charges you with its mouth open. Then it swallows you whole!

The End

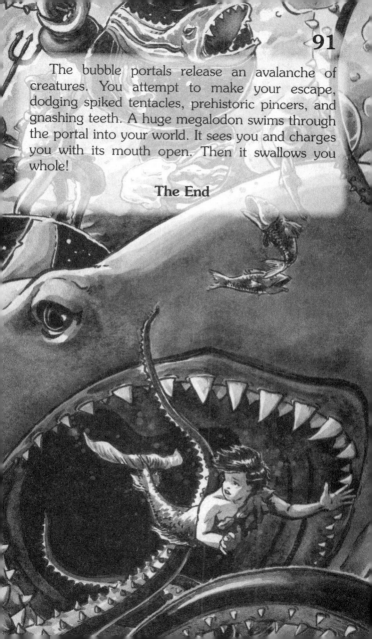

"Fine," you tell Zyzi. "I'll help you capture Mika."

Zyzi grabs a net made of blue shiny scales, and together you sneak closer to Mika and toss it over him.

Suddenly, Mika's face changes from soft to hard scales. His blue eyes turn black, and his mouth fills with rows of sharp teeth. Mika's tiny body starts to transform into a huge sea monster. "*ROAAAAAR*," Mika yells against the glowing net, but it holds fast and Mika changes back into a sea slug. You and Zyzi haul the net into a giant clam and lock Mika inside.

"Mika is the ghost of the sea monster at the bottom of the Abyss, a dangerous and powerful creature. It will be safer for him to be contained this way." Zyzi rummages around his shelves and makes some adjustments to a pair of goggles. He hands them to you and says that he has modified these goggles to give you the ability to see the Eye wherever it is.

You take the glasses and put them on. Zyzi whistles and a goblin shark arrives at the mouth of his cave. You jump onto the shark and zoom toward Brooklyn.

Go on to the next page.

The goblin shark is fast, and you pass the Atlantean guards in a blur. Toward the surface, a school of shimmering tunas starts to follow you. Their shiny scales make rainbows in the blue water.

You take this as a good omen. *It was worth betraying an ally to save my family,* you think. Sometimes you must make tough decisions, but your rise to the surface wouldn't be this magical if capturing Mika had been a mistake. . . .

The goblin shark drops you off outside Rockaway Beach and starts chasing the tunas. You reach your hand out to break the surface and scan the horizon, but something catches your tail. You look back and see a huge net trawling toward you. It's bright and shiny, but when it gets closer you realize it contains all the flashing tunas. The net envelops you and pulls you to the surface.

You have been caught by a commercial fishing vessel. It spells . . .

The End

Just as you are about to get out of your seats and swim toward the sea dragon's mouth, a flash of blue zaps the tracks. The seatbelt bar locks into place and the coaster lurches forward.

"Wait, what's that noise?" you ask, and you and Rabbit look at each other anxiously.

The rumbling gets louder. "The ride is reanimating!" Rabbit shouts. The roar of animatronic creatures echoes through the tunnel. Rabbit screams when a fake shark jumps out at her and gnashes its jaws!

The ride is so old that the set pieces start to fall apart. The shark's teeth tumble out of its mouth like a pair of dentures and narrowly miss Rabbit. The set pieces fall like anchors behind you. The coaster dives deep in a series of spiraling curves, mimicking a maelstrom, picking up even more speed. You and Rabbit scream and pull at the bar as the coaster dives deeper. The weighted first car causes your coaster to pick up more and more speed. Soon the coaster is barely keeping to the tracks.

Go on to the next page.

You feel the tracks start to vibrate and you look over your shoulder. The rusty tracks behind you are snapping from the weight of the coaster.

"Look up ahead!" Rabbit screams. You turn around and see a second sea dragon mouth, but this time it's not a tunnel, it's a painting on a brick wall. You and Rabbit scream and pull at the bar, but it holds tight. You hear the screech and rumble of another coaster behind you. You hit the wall in a shower of bubbles. The force of the collision reverberates through the old park, causing the deteriorating ride to collapse.

In a rush of bubbles and fleeing fish, the Mystical Mermaid crumbles into a pile of rubble, trapping you and Rabbit in a watery grave.

The End

The ride controls are waterlogged: there's no way you can get this ride to work.

"What now?" you say to Rabbit.

"Want to return to the parade and do some more sleuthing at the surface?"

You are on your way back to the parade when Rabbit spots a pink and green boat chugging toward the crowd. "Can you eat human food?" Rabbit asks. She points to a sign on the boat that reads, **TODAY'S SPECIAL: SEAWEED ICE CREAM!** You nod enthusiastically.

You and Rabbit swim toward the boat. A Strider with pink hair and a green moustache leans toward you. "Wow, those costumes look so real!" says Pinky of Pinky's Ice Cream Skiff. "I think you might have my favorite costumes of the day, so free ice cream for you! Would you like to try our Seaweed Special?"

Rabbit says no, she'll have the Starfish Strawberry. Pinky gives her two heaping scoops.

"And how about you, what would you like?"

You look at the menu options: there is everything from Azul Apple Cider to Sea Zebra Chocolate, but nothing sounds as good as the Seaweed Special.

You point at the Seaweed Special and Pinky grins. They hand you three scoops. The ice cream is dark green and filled with crunchy caramel seaweed bits. It is delicious! You thank Pinky, and the two of you take a break from your quest to enjoy your ice cream.

The End

You choose not to clean up the shrine, and instead you swim around the statue. This Snariadne statue looks much older than the one in Merzood City. The carvings and symbols are more complicated, and the jewel on her crown has been removed. A white spotlight turns on behind you. You whip around and get momentarily blinded by its brightness.

A net falls over you and drags you through the darkness, into a decompression chamber and then into a holding cell.

"Hello? Who's there? Help!" you call, thrashing around wildly. You notice that your tail is transforming into legs, and your gills are disappearing. When you open your eyes again you see the faces of two shocked Striders.

"Who are you? *What* are you?" one of them asks.

"I'm . . . I'm Neru," you say hesitantly. "I'm a member of the Merzood clan."

Their eyes widen even more. "Hello, Neru. I'm the captain of the *Seeker*," says the taller of the two.

"The *Seeker*?" you ask, thinking of your old life, seeking in the reef outside Merzood City. You feel a pang of sadness.

"It's a deep-sea exploration submarine. We're scientists."

"Oh," you say. "Can you give me a ride home?"

The shorter one shakes his head. "I'm afraid not, Neru. You see . . . you're our greatest discovery yet!"

The End

"I have a bad feeling about that tunnel," you say. "Something about it doesn't feel right."

You take out the map and look it over. There is a faint trail that leads away from the ride and back to Aqua Park. You and Rabbit swim back through the tracks and out of the Mystical Mermaid. The electric-blue fish swim past you. It seems like they want you to follow, but you keep swimming toward the parade.

You swim past the Wonder Wheel and the Cyclone, and reenter Aqua Park. The parade is in full swing.

Turn to page 66.

You choose to participate in the swimming competition, and you follow all the participants to the boardwalk. Everyone lines up and the coast guard explains the course—it is a one-lap sprint around a red buoy. The first one back to the boardwalk wins.

All the participants line up on the edge of the boardwalk and take their positions. You are so excited to win the crown that you haven't really thought this contest through. The whistle blows and you dive in, but as soon as you dip your head underwater, your legs transform back into your long tail.

"A mermaid! A real mermaid!" a participant screams. Everyone on the boardwalk turns to you, and though you're already rounding the buoy, you know you can't return to the boardwalk now that you've exposed your identity to the Striders. You are forced to swim back to Atlantis empty-handed.

The End

100

Artistry and inventions feel so natural to you, there's no way you'll lose! All the contestants line up on the pirate ship, and a huge pile of recyclable goods is loaded onto the ship. When the buzzer goes off you dive in, taking everything that seems usable: cans, wire, string, and more. You let the materials guide what you're making. The Merzood magic flows, and at the end of the competition you've created a breathing apparatus out of recycled materials.

All the participants present their inventions to the judges. As you survey the entries, one catches your eye: it is a life jacket made with upcycled materials. The artist who created the piece is wearing an incredible lobster outfit and has flaming orange hair. "I'm Madame Decopada," she announces, presenting her life jacket to the judges.

"And I'm Neru," you say, handing over your breathing apparatus.

"Look at this craftsmanship!" one of the judges says, her eyes flitting back and forth between your and Madame Decopada's creations. "I think we'll need to put these to the test."

"Can you try this for me?" you ask a nearby spectator dressed in an octopus costume, while Madame Decopada finds her own volunteer to test her life jacket. The octopus nods enthusiastically and jumps into the water. The breathing apparatus works! Madame Decopada's life jacket works too, so the judges move you both on to the next stage of the competition: singing.

Go on to the next page.

You, Madame Decopada, and the winner of the swimming competition take the stage on the pirate ship. Madame Decopada goes first and performs a sea shanty. The crowd goes wild.

You're up after Madame Decopada and when you take the stage you feel nervous. You don't know any Strider songs, so you sing an old Merzood song. As soon as you start singing, sea creatures start to join the crowd. You watch as schools of fish, crabs, and a pod of dolphins join the Striders. At the end of your song, the fish flip and the dolphins squeak.

Suddenly, a group of triangular fins approaches the crowd, and someone screams "SHARK!" All the Striders scatter. In the chaos, you grab the Mermaid Queen crown, dive into the water, and swim toward your home reef. There's a flash of green, and a manta ray pulls up beside you. The guards cuff you and take you back to the Court of High Seas where the Ruler is waiting.

"Here is the Eye," you say, and toss the Ruler the Mermaid Queen crown. "Now let my family go free!"

The Ruler grins. "Congratulations, Neruvid. I have to admit that I didn't expect you to succeed. But it looks like you really are the best of the seekers. GUARDS!" he yells suddenly.

"Wait, what are you doing?" you shout as your arms are seized from behind.

"Oh, Neruvid," the Ruler says. "You'll be staying right here with me, as my permanent treasure seeker. I'll let your family out one of these days . . . I promise . . ."

The End

You grab the invention with the purple sparks. When you unwrap it, you see a place to put your finger in the center of it. Two arrows are pointing in opposite directions, and there is a red button with a question mark on it. You play with the arrows and the button, but they don't do anything.

Suddenly, a huge Atlantean guard breaks down the door. The guard's eyes are white and blank, and he growls in a robotic voice, "You are safe, please follow me."

As the guard approaches, you press the buttons to no avail. The Atlantean guard swipes at you and you duck. You press your finger into the center of the invention and it finally comes to life. You press the question mark button, and in a flash you are falling through a tunnel of blue shining bubbles, traveling through space and time.

Turn to the next page.

104

As you travel through the portal, you feel your tail changing, transforming into Strider legs. You land with a *thud!* and steady yourself on the stage in front of you. The device chirps, "Coney Island, 1923!"

"Welcome to the world-famous Coney Island Sideshow! The strangest show on Earth!" a ringleader in a red suit announces. Performers cross the stage, flipping and fire-eating. The audience is filled with admiration, gasping at the spectacle. The crowd looks like old photos of Striders you've seen in your encyclopedia fragments.

"Now for the main event," says the ringleader. The lights slowly dim to a deep blue. "Legends tell of mer-creatures living in the waters around Brooklyn! Deep in the waves live these bizarre, scale-covered creatures. Beauty or monster? See for yourself!"

The ringleader snaps his fingers, and a curtain opens to a flash of blue light. In the light you see the silhouette of a Strider torso and a tail. . . .

The device beeps and you are pulled back into the swirling bubble portal.

Turn to page 106.

106

In a bubbly flash you land on your feet in a Strider neighborhood you've never seen before. The device says, "Graves End, Brooklyn, 2025."

It's a peaceful neighborhood with a big creepy house. You look down the road and see a station wagon pull up. A family arrives at the house. "We're here, Rabbit!" says Rabbit's mom as Rabbit leaps out of the car with a white cat and a red backpack.

The device beeps and sends you forward in time to the same block. "Graves End, Brooklyn, 2052." The sky is dark and rumbling. You see the same family rushing out of the house and putting stuff in the car, but this time Rabbit and her family are much older, and she helps her parents into the car.

You hear the roar of rushing water, and an enormous dark wave rushes over the neighborhood toward Rabbit and her family. Suddenly a blue bubble surrounds them. The wall of water crashes over the protective bubble and the rest of the neighborhood.

In the bright blue light, you see two Merzoods on either side of Rabbit's family. You recognize them: it is your Auntie Quell and Auntie Echo!

The device beeps and pulls you back into the swirling tunnel.

Turn to page 109.

108

You dive into one of the giant clams and slam its shell shut. You can hear the submarine whirring above you. You peek out of the clam and see bubbles all around you. A yellow submarine with the name *Seeker* painted on the side slowly swims around the wreck. The bubbles from the *Seeker*'s propeller fill the giant clam's mouth and it starts to wiggle. It almost feels like it's about to sneeze!

"Please don't sneeze!" you whisper to the giant clam, but the clam hiccups and you fly out, landing in front of the *Seeker*. In a flash, the scientists on the *Seeker* take photos and videos. They try to catch you with a robotic arm, but you manage to slip away and escape into the wreck. Reports of a "Brooklyn Mermaid" circulate throughout the Strider world. More submarines start to visit the area and all the creatures are forced into hiding.

The End

"Brooklyn Bridge, 2275!" chirps the invention. You are perched dangerously on the top column of the Brooklyn Bridge, but the bridge is submerged under hundreds of feet of water! Ocean spray hits as you fall forward slightly, but you catch yourself.

The device whirrs again and you're pulled back into the swirling bubble vortex.

Turn to page 111.

You splash back into the ocean. "Merzood City, Jurassic era," the invention beeps.

You look around nervously. According to your encyclopedia, the Jurassic era was the time of sea monsters. You hope you don't meet any Thalassiodracons. The water is much warmer and the animals that swim around you are different from anything you've ever seen. Ammonites and piranha-like fish swim by you. The plants are extraordinarily colorful, and the water is so clear.

You look around for any signs of Merzood life and a blue flash catches your eye. You swim toward it, and through a forest of thick, tree-like kelp you find a circular clearing. In the clearing you see a stone carving of Snariadne. In Snariadne's crown is a bright blue stone with a darker stone at the center. "It must be the Eye!" you think. You reach out to grab it, but the device beeps and sends you back in a rush of bubbles.

Turn to the next page.

112

"Merzood City, 2083," the device chirps, and it feels good to be home. The Atlantean guard that attacked you before you time-traveled is guarding the door. He rushes at you when you return and growls, "Your safety depends on your ability to comply. Place your weapon on the ground . . ."

You look at the device and think of your next move. You definitely won't be complying, but maybe you could use it to go back to this morning and make a different choice? Maybe with this device, you could look for the Eye in Brooklyn! But then you see the red question mark button and you wonder where that could take you next.

If you choose to press the question mark button, turn to page 117.

If you choose to use the device to start your quest over, turn to page 126.

You gather all your power before you reply. "Shut your clam, Zyzi, I refuse to make that choice!" you say. Zyzi turns on you, eyes glowing with pink flames.

You walk over to Zyzi's wall of potions and creatures caught in jars. You knock them over and break all the jars. All manner of mythic creatures rise up in the cave: sea dragons, a bubble-snorting Pega-sea horse, octopuses with rainbow legs, and glittering jellyfish! Before they attack, Zyzi throws a potion at you, and in a pink flash you are traveling through a tunnel of tentacles. . . .

Turn to the next page.

114

You cough and shake your head. You feel strange, different somehow. You open your eyes and look around. You see a piece of pink plastic coral and a treasure chest bubbling open and closed. The ground is littered with green and blue rocks.

Beyond the coral is a blurry room where a blurry Strider is moving around. You swim closer and hit your face against glass. Then you catch a glimpse of your reflection. You have orange fins, a long tail, and black bulging eyes. You scream and a stream of bubbles forms in front of you. You are filled with horror as it dawns on you: Zyzi has trapped you in the body of a pet goldfish!

The End

You wish you had the courage to join Ximz and the Bottom-Feeders. Sometimes the things we want to do can scare us, but you realize that art and music always come from curiosity, risk-taking, and even failure.

As you watch the Bottom-Feeders play, you feel a deep sense of longing. You wish you were on the stage with them. You feel frustration well up inside you. Then you start thinking about your Aunties and the Eye. If you don't put yourself out there, how are you going to save them?

You swim away from the Bottom-Feeders as tears well up in your eyes. You start exploring the wreck and swim into the bowels of the ship. Seeking makes you feel a little better. In the bottom of the ship, you explore the living quarters and find a locked room. There is a glowing blue light coming from under the door. You grab a pole and wrench it open.

The blue glow reminds you of the Eye, but instead of the legendary stone, it is a swarm of box jellyfish! Their tentacles wrap around you like fingers, stinging you in the blue glow.

The End

116

Knowing your family, that "DON'T PRESS THE BUTTON" warning might mean a prank, but the guards don't know that! "WAIT!" you shout, holding up the device where they can see it. "When I press this button, this device will call a creature from the Kelp Forest!"

The guards exchange nervous looks. The Kelp Forest has a lot of cursed lore about it. As a Merzood, you know that the legends are probably untrue, but the Atlantean guards don't know that!

In a flash, you toss the invention across the room and chaos ensues; the guards scatter and hit the floor. In the shuffle you swim out of the front door. You don't have much time before the guards realize you outsmarted them!

If you choose to swim deeper into Merzood City, turn to page 118.

If you choose to hide from the guards in the Kelp Forest, turn to page 119.

You press the red question mark button, and the device pulls you through the tunnel of bubbles. You land in an odd position; it feels like you're lying down, but you're not comfortable. Bright blue lights flash in your eyes and you hear the rustle of a curtain.

The familiar voice of the ringleader bellows over the stage: "Legends tell of mer-creatures living in the waters around Brooklyn! Deep in the waves live the mythical, scale-covered creatures. Beauty or monster? See for yourself!" The ringleader snaps his fingers and two stagehands push you to center stage.

"For the first time in history, the Brooklyn Mermaid!"

The ringleader raises his arm with a flourish. A blue spotlight shines in your eyes and a faceless crowd goes wild. Performers dressed as fish flip and dip around you. The crowd erupts into applause.

The End

118

You swim deeper into Merzood City. Usually bustling with activity, the city is now a ghost town. In the city center is a shrine for Snariadne, the Merzood spirit of chance. The shrine is unusually messy and covered in garbage. You clean it up but notice that it has been vandalized. The jewel in Snariadne's crown is gone and her arm is missing. Suddenly you feel a pair of cuffs snap over your wrists. You turn around and see the green glowing eyes of an Atlantean guard. The guard hauls you onto a manta ray and takes you back to the Atlantean fortress. They lock you in the dungeon because you violated the terms of your exile.

In the dungeon, you have a bittersweet reunion with your Aunties. You hug each other tightly in the sea cave dungeon, wishing you were free. How will you ever get back home to your Hideaway?

The End

You swim into the Kelp Forest, ignoring the signs at the entrance with **DANGER** symbols scrawled in Merzood. This forest has always been talked about in a whisper—there's lots of lore about how it is home to a sea witch. You don't really believe that story. Plus, the forest is a perfect place to hide from the guards.

The guards approach the forest but they don't dare enter it. You hide behind a thicket of kelp and try to keep your breathing even. Eventually, the guards move on.

You wait until you hear the mantas take off, and then swim along the edge of the Kelp Forest. After a few fin flicks, you spy another Atlantean guard swimming suspiciously with a large wheel that looks like it may open a hatch. Maybe following the guard could help you find your Aunties?

If you choose to travel deeper into the Kelp Forest, turn to page 121.

If you choose to follow the Atlantean guard, turn to page 124.

You swim deeper into the Kelp Forest. No reason to risk another run-in with the Atlantean guards! As you drift through the long blades of kelp, the forest becomes increasingly dense and dark. You start to wonder whether you are getting closer to land.

You pump your tail and swim up to the surface. You can see the lights of the Strider world just a few miles away. It's so beautiful, especially the way the lights play off the water.

Suddenly you hear the buzz of a motor. You turn around just in time to see a tugboat headed right for you. You try to dodge it, but the side hits your head and knocks you out. You sink back into the kelp.

Turn to page 123.

You don't know how long you floated in the kelp before someone rescued you. The sound of bottles clinking wakes you up. Your sight is blurry at first, and you rub your eyes. There's a huge wall of potions, different colored bubbles contained in jars, Strider possessions, carvings, and a large white catfish in the corner. The catfish watches you intently.

In the center of the room, a Merzood empties bottles into large bowl. She has long purple hair and a blue tail. She walks over to you and puts a slimy compress on your head. The compress smells terrible and makes you cringe. You feel so weak that you fall asleep again.

When you wake up again you feel much stronger. You swim up and look around. The Merzood swims back in to meet you. "My name is Mirra," she says. You notice a blue ring on her hand. It looks like she's wearing the same ring as you and your Aunties.

"I'm Neru. Thank you for rescuing me!" you say.

"How did I come to find you floating in the forest?" asks Mirra. You pause before you answer. Maybe you should lie? You aren't sure how honest you can be with her. . . .

If you choose to lie to Mirra, turn to page 38.

If you choose to tell Mirra the truth, turn to page 127.

124

You follow the Atlantean guard at a safe distance. After a few fin flicks, you see him stop at a rock wall that looks completely normal. Then the guard inserts the large wheel into a groove in the wall and turns it to the right three times. A secret hatch opens in the rock.

Suddenly, a seal attacks the Atlantean guard and snaps him up in her jaws. She stops and looks at you, winks, and zooms off to another part of the reef. Now the Atlantean hideout is open and unguarded.

Go on to the next page.

You dash to the secret passageway and peek inside. You hear creatures rushing back and forth. A flash of lightning illuminates hundreds of eels swimming around a glowing green orb. The eels' eyes are green and they look exhausted. It doesn't seem like they're allowed to stop swimming. The eels are wearing collars that conduct their electrical current into the stone and charge it. You realize this must be how the Ruler is powering the Atlantean fortress.

If you choose to release the eels,
turn to page 132.

If you choose not to release the eels,
turn to page 41.

126

You decide to restart your quest, and you program the invention to take you back to the Court of High Seas. You fiddle with the keys and the invention chirps, "Court of High Seas, 2083." You fly through the bubble portal and land with a thud on the sea cave floor, but you're at the back of the crowd and no one seems to have noticed your arrival.

"Order! Order!" snaps the Ruler of Atlantis, banging his gavel.

You watch as the guards rip the blindfold off you—the you from this morning, you guess—and the Ruler makes his speech. The image of the Eye is brought in and the Ruler gives you your choice. You know what your answer will be, and now's your chance to change your fate! You could make a disturbance and distract the court, or you could attempt to free your other self before the guards drop you into the Abyss.

*If you choose to make a disturbance,
turn to page 45.*

*If you choose to free yourself,
turn to page 43.*

"I swam into the Kelp Forest to escape the Atlantean guards," you say. "The Ruler of Atlantis kidnapped my Aunties. He won't let them go unless I find the Eye, an old Atlantean treasure."

"The Eye," Mirra says, shaking her head. "I may be about to blow your mind, but the Eye is not an ancient Atlantean treasure. It is a Merzood power source, and it has the power to control all the light in the ocean . . ."

"What?" you cry. "I've never heard that. My Aunties have taught me everything they know!"

You stop to wonder. Have they? Did they keep secrets for your own protection?

"The Ruler has always wanted control of the Merzoods," Mirra explains. "We get our power from the ocean's light and her currents. And that source is both huge and endless. If the Atlanteans gain power over the Eye, they will change the oceans forever." Mirra draws a breath and takes a stone carving out of her collection. "Let me teach you to harness Merzood powers and save your family. Then you won't have to give the Eye to the Ruler . . ."

You agree immediately.

You become Mirra's apprentice and learn how to use Merzood bubble portals to travel through time and space. To create a bubble you must first call the Merzood ancestors and ask them for their assistance.

Turn to the next page.

128

One night you wake up to find Mirra desperately making portal after portal. You watch her walk into a portal, jump out, destroy it, and make a new one. It's as if she's trying to access a certain place in time. Mirra hears you come into her room and sighs, "I have been trying to locate your Aunties, but something is blocking my portals from reaching them. I've tried everything, and I don't think the ancestors want to hear from me anymore!" Mirra sits down and plays with her ring.

Go on to the next page.

"Let's take a break and go somewhere else?" she asks, and you agree. You and Mirra join hands and call forth a frothing bubble. You both step into it.

You go back in time. Your younger Aunties and Mirra are painting together on a colorful sunlit reef. "This is the last time we were together before the Atlanteans attacked us. This is the last time that everything felt normal." Mirra sighs, and you see her younger self present your Aunties with a small box of shiny blue rings. Your Aunties each pick one and put them on. After all three of them have put their rings on, they hold them together like a trio of superheroes. Then they fall back laughing on the reef.

At that moment, a squadron of manta rays rockets over the reef toward Merzood City. They encircle the city and descend on the Merzoods in a surprise attack. Your Aunties and Mirra watch helplessly as a green glow washes over the city.

"We need to hide in the Kelp Forest," Mirra tells your Aunties in a low voice.

"No!" Auntie Echo replies sternly. "We need to go back to the city and help!"

"There's no point," Mirra answers. "It's too late."

"I refuse to sit by and watch my city fall into ruin," Auntie Quell says, and the note in her voice is final. Auntie Echo agrees, and Mirra nods at them sadly before she turns away.

You watch helplessly as Mirra swims into the Kelp Forest and your Aunties sneak back into the city, now a battleground.

The End

In the darkness, the Atlantean fortress descends into chaos. The fortress is a maze, but you're an excellent solver of puzzles and mazes. Your intuition tells you to swim into a small sea cave tunnel. There is a faint light at the end of it. The tunnel has its own current that sweeps you through the fortress, flowing faster and faster until it ends at a vent. You crash through the vent and slam into an Atlantean guard, knocking him out cold. You grab his trident and swim through the labyrinthine corridors to the dungeons.

You swim down a very dark corridor and a winding tunnel. At the end of the tunnel, you see a flash of blue and bubbles popping in the darkness.

"Auntie Echo? Auntie Quell?" you whisper into the dark.

"Neru?!" Auntie Echo calls back. You swim down the corridor, and finally you and your Aunties hug in the darkness.

"We can't use bubble portals to get out of here because we're still cuffed!" Auntie Quell says. You use the trident you stole from the guard to shatter the cuffs in a bright flash of green.

You and your Aunties join hands and hum together. A blue light appears between you and a bubble portal begins to form. It's enormous! In the light of the blue bubble, you see the faces of all the freed prisoners. When the bubble portal is ready, your family and the rest of the prisoners jump in and travel back to Merzood City.

The End

132

You watch the eels swim and wonder how you can release them. It seems like the green stone has a hypnotic power over them. Maybe if you remove the stone it will break the connection? You dive underneath the eels, hugging the walls of the sea cave. You dodge and duck your way to the center of the swarm. Skirting the occasional tail, you use the sea cave floor to propel yourself into the glowing stone and grab it.

The sea cave goes dark. You hear the eels slowly stop swimming, and in the flickering light of the orb you can see their eyes returning to normal. The eels shake their heads and look around, confused. One of them sees the open hatch and takes off. The others follow and soon the sea cave is empty.

Now that you've cut the power to the Atlantean fortress, the Ruler is vulnerable. The guards will be surprised by the power outage, and you'll finally be able to swim through the fortress undetected. In the chaos, anything is possible! You could release your Aunties or take over the Atlantean kingdom. Saving your Aunties is your primary mission, but the idea of taking over the kingdom is tempting, especially because it would start a revolution.

If you choose to take over the Atlantean kingdom, turn to page 30.

If you choose to release your family, turn to page 131.

ABOUT THE ARTIST

Illustrator: Gabhor Utomo was born in Indonesia. He moved to California to pursue his passion in art. He received his degree from Academy of Art University in San Francisco in spring 2003. Since graduation, he's worked as a freelance illustrator and has illustrated a number of children's books. Gabhor lives with his wife, Dina, and his twin girls in Portland, Oregon.

ABOUT THE AUTHOR

C. E. Simpson was born in a hospital that no longer exists. They grew up on the coast of Brooklyn, where they learned the legends and stories of the Merzood Mer-people. They are a non-binary artist, beachcomber, and interactive writer.

C. E. Simpson would like to acknowledge the indigenous people of the Lenape nation, the original caretakers of the area now known as Brooklyn, and currently our greatest climate activists.

For games, activities, and other fun stuff, or to write to C. E. Simpson, visit us online at CYOA.com